FARAWAY DRUMS

BY
VIRGINIA KROLL

ILLUSTRATED BY
FLOYD COOPER

Little, Brown and Company
Boston   New York   Toronto   London

To Andi Hummel, my faraway friend
⊹ V. K. ⊹

For Jackie
⊹ F. C. ⊹

First Edition

Library of Congress Cataloging-in-Publication Data

Kroll, Virginia L.
    Faraway drums / by Virginia Kroll ; illustrated by Floyd Cooper.
        p.   cm.
    Summary: Jamila and her little sister are frightened by the loud city noises at their
new apartment, but they find comfort in recalling the stories their great-grandma used
to tell about life in Africa.
    ISBN 0-316-50449-1
    [1. Afro-Americans — Fiction.   2. Sisters — Fiction.   3. Africa — Fiction.   4. City and
town life — Fiction.]   I. Cooper, Floyd, ill.   II. Title.
PZ7.K9227Far 1998
[E] — dc20   95-14517

10 9 8 7 6 5 4 3 2 1

SC

Published simultaneously in Canada by Little, Brown & Company (Canada) Limited

The illustrations for this book were painted in oil wash on board. The text was set in
Poppl-Pontifex. The display lines were set in Hoffman. The book was printed and
bound in Hong Kong by South China Printing.

Here's me, Jamila Jefferson, not even used to the idea of movin' yet, let alone actually livin' here. And already Mama is leavin' me in charge.

I get right home from school, just like Mama told me when I left this mornin'. "You know I gotta get to work, soon as you step inside," she said.

Before my backpack is even off my shoulder, Mama tells me, "Mind your little sister and stay locked in. You'll be safe that way."

I thud my backpack onto the floor. Mama frowns.

"Mrs. Harris is right next door if you need her, remember," Mama tells me. "She'll be by now and then to look in on you. Wait till she says her name before you go opening that door."

"This is a nasty place," I mumble.

Mama hears me and says real fast, "No better, no worse than anyplace we ever lived." Then she wraps Zakiya and me in our spider hug, tight and warm, and we are all arms around each other.

But then she has to go.

I lock up behind her.

My sister stands on tiptoe at the window and watches Mama walk to the bus stop. Her shoulders sink. I feel it, too.

"I'm not likin' this," Zakiya says for both of us.

When Mama turns the corner, we go away from the window. I try to do my homework, but the shadows are gettin' darker and the sounds outside are gettin' louder. Somebody knocks on the door across the hall. We hear it clear, 'cause the walls are thin.

"I'm scared, Jamila," Zakiya says.

Me, too, I think. But I say nothin', 'cause I am in charge.

There is more knockin', then bangin'. The thumpin' gets fiercer, and Zakiya starts her cryin'.

My heart is thumpin', too, like a scared rabbit's. But I take a deep breath and close my eyes, just like my great-gramma taught me. I shoo the scared rabbit away and imagine a proud drum poundin' in its place. I feel the Africa inside me.

"Hush," I tell Zakiya.

"But the bangin' makes me scared," she says.

I wipe her tears with my sleeve and sit her down on the sofa. "Listen," I tell her. "It's just drums. The drummer is beatin' out a message. Shhh…"

I whisper in a faraway voice, 'cause I am listenin', too. Listenin' to the stories Great-gramma put in my ears before she died, stories 'bout Africa, where her people, my people, began. I hear raindrops sizzlin' on sun-scorched soil and a herd of wildebeests thunderin'. I close my eyes again and see a reed hut by a river and fat brown babies splashin'.

Me and Zakiya, we listen together. The drummin' outside gets soft, till we hear *thump, thump, rum, pum,* every beat farther away than the one before.

I got to tell Zakiya like Great-gramma told me. "Listen to the faraway drums," I say.

Zakiya whines, "Oh, Ja-MIL-a." But she isn't cryin' anymore.

The sun goes down, and we eat our canned spaghetti. I tell Zakiya it is *fou-fou,* just like they eat in West Africa. She giggles and says, "Oh, Ja-MIL-a," again.

But then we jump, 'cause there is a whoopin' and a howlin' down in the street. A car door slams shut, squeaks open, slams again. More voices.

"Hyenas," I say, tryin' to keep the shakin' out of my voice. "Bickerin' over the scraps they found."

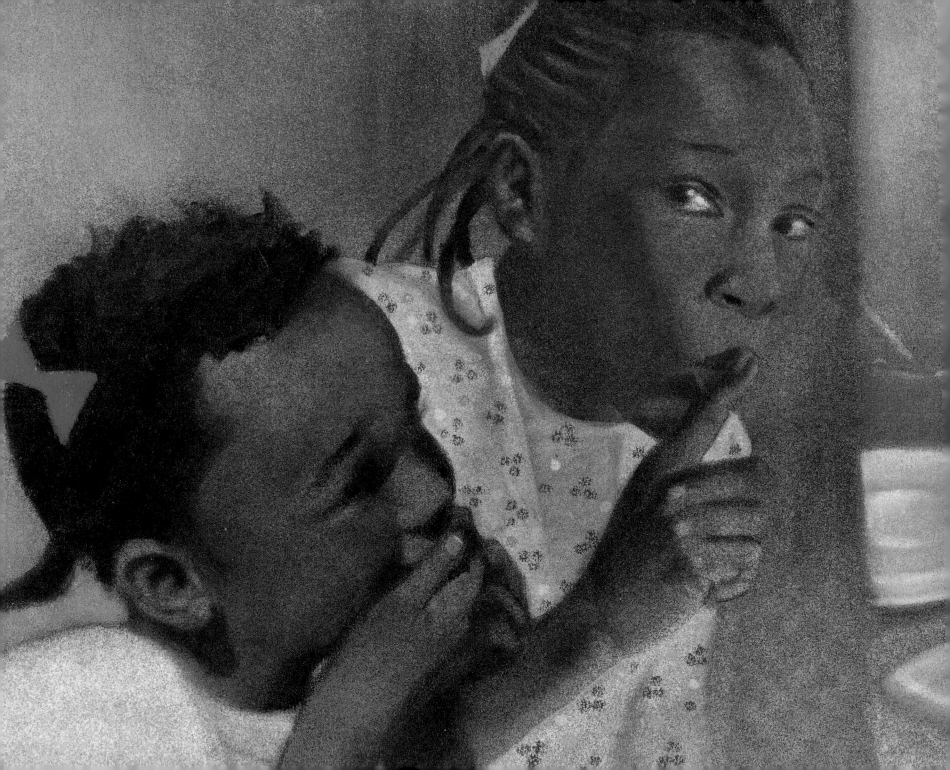

Another car pulls up, with screamin' brakes and a trumpetin' horn. I tell Zakiya, "Elephants, come to the waterin' hole. Listen to that one. Must be a bull with eight-foot-long ivory tusks!"

I give Zakiya her doll so she'll be still while I tidy the kitchen. I try to sing her a song, just like Great-gramma used to sing to me. But a baby's cryin' next door, screams travelin' right through the walls.

"Why's that baby carryin' on so?" Zakiya asks.

"Got into a nest of red ants and got stung bad, I 'magine," I tell her.

"Ouch," says Zakiya, like it's happenin' right to her.

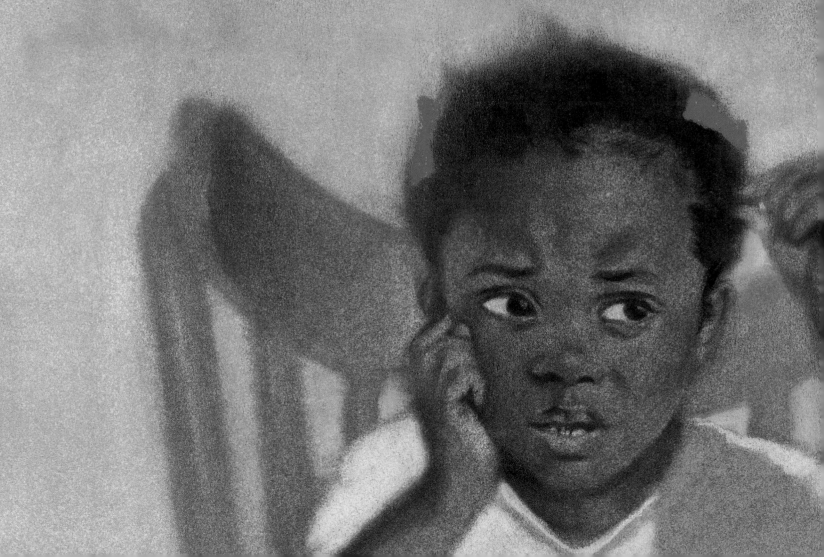

I finish up the dishes. Zakiya pesters me to read to her before bed. We sit on the sofa, and I read one book, then another. Zakiya wants to hear a third, but I say no.

She starts to sass me but stops real quick when she hears sirens screechin' 'round the corner. I'm used to sirens, but not Zakiya. They still upset her some.

"Sirens!" she cries, clingin' to me tight, her book droppin' on the floor. I touch her mouth to make her hush and point way up. "Monkeys," I say, "high in the treetops. Fightin' over a juicy cocoa pod."

"Monkeys?" She looks up, almost like she sees.

There is a gentle tappin' at our door.

"Yes?" I say, the door lock tight in my hand.

"It's Mrs. Harris," comes the voice from the hall.

I recognize it and unlock the door. Mrs. Harris strolls in with her print dress swishin' and her ear hoops janglin'. I feel safe just lookin' at her.

"How you girls doin'?" she asks.

"Just fine," I say. "Just fine, thanks."

"Won't be long now till your mama is home," Mrs. Harris says.

After she leaves, the safe feelin' stays. The designs on her dress are still dancin' in front of my eyes, bright as photo flashes.

"The head woman," I pretend, "come to our hut with her *kente* cloth robe." Zakiya gets out her crayons and draws a picture of Mrs. Harris and her dress. She uses every color in the box.

"Zakiya, come on, girl," I say when it is time for bed. "The Zambezi River is flowin', warm and gentle. Come, get under the waterfall." And Zakiya, who always argues "NO BATH" till me and Mama are fed up, gets undressed and jumps right in.

After, she lies on the sofa in her purple pajamas, smellin' sweet. The corridor is quiet for a change, and there is no commotion in the street.

Zakiya falls asleep, and I get to do some homework. I hear the *hrr-hrr-hrr* of her sound-asleep breathin'. "Little lioness purrin'," I say, and make a den with a blanket to keep her snug.

But then her dreams explode. A stampede of footsteps is runnin', stompin',
clompin' up and down the hall, up and down the stairs.
Zakiya bolts up, her eyes wide. I sit tense and still.

The drums of my people pound in my chest again. But I have run out of stories to tell my little sister. We listen, me and Zakiya, till the footsteps go out the door and down the street, leaving their echoes in our ears.

Zakiya lies down. "Zebras," she says sleepily. "A whole herd."

And just before she goes back to sleep, I see the Africa in her eyes. . . .